BEGINNER READER

RAINBOW magic™

A Fairy Ballet

Orchard Beginner Readers are specially created to develop
literacy skills, confidence and a love of reading.

ORCHARD BOOKS

First published in the USA in 2013 by Scholastic Inc
This edition published in Great Britain in 2017 by The Watts Publishing Group

1 3 5 7 9 10 8 6 4 2

© 2017 Rainbow Magic Limited.
© 2017 HIT Entertainment Limited.
Illustrations copyright © Orchard Books, 2017

HiT entertainment

A CIP catalogue record for this book is available from the British Library.

ISBN 978 1 40834 581 8

Printed in China

The paper and board used in this book are made from wood from responsible sources

Orchard Books
An imprint of Hachette Children's Group
Part of The Watts Publishing Group Limited
Carmelite House, 50 Victoria Embankment, London EC4Y 0DZ

An Hachette UK Company
www.hachette.co.uk
www.hachettechildrens.co.uk

Crystal
the Snow
Fairy

Evie
the Mist
Fairy

Abigail
the Breeze
Fairy

Meet the Weather Fairies

The Weather Fairies have a treat
in store for you. It's time to
join them on an adventure!

Goldie
the Sunshine
Fairy

Storm the
Lightning
Fairy

Pearl
the Cloud
Fairy

Hayley
the Rain
Fairy

It's early morning in Fairyland, and the Weather Fairies are just waking up. There's a loud knock at their door. "Who could it be?" Crystal wonders.

Storm opens the door, and a frog strides in.
It's Bertram, the royal messenger.

"Hello, Weather Fairies," Bertram says.
"I have an invitation from the Fairy
Godmother for you."
"The Fairy Godmother?" gasps Evie.

Goldie opens the envelope and reads:

Dear fairies and friends:
Come one, come all!
In Fairyland, we will have a ball.
With songs and skits
for the king and queen,
it will be a celebration
like you've never seen.
Please be sure to prepare your part.
Bring a gift straight from your heart.
It's a night of fun for all to share.
I hope that I will see you there.

Always,
Fairy Godmother

"Oh, it sounds wonderful," sighs Hayley.
"But what about the gift?" Abigail asks.

"The Fairy Godmother wants the guests to
perform for the king and queen," Bertram
explains. "That will be your gift. Remember,
it needs to be from the heart."

The Weather Fairies look at one another.
"Have a good day," Bertram says. "See you
at the party."

"I can't believe we get to perform for the king and queen," says Crystal.

"What shall we do?" Goldie says.

"It has to be from the heart," Hayley reminds her fairy friends.

Just then, the sound of a beautiful song comes through the window.

"Let's go outside," suggests Crystal.

"We do our best thinking there."

Outside, the fairies see a robin.
"Was that your pretty song?" Pearl
asks the bird.

The bird chirps and flies toward the forest.
The fairies follow.

"I love to hear the breeze whisper," Abigail says, when the fairies stop for a rest.
"I love how things look magical in the mist," says Evie.

"I love snowflakes," says Crystal. "When I watch them whirl around, I want to dance."
"We all love weather," Goldie says.
"Maybe that can be our gift."

"How?" asks Storm.
"We can dance to show everyone how weather makes us feel," says Goldie.
"We can create a ballet!" Evie exclaims.

All the fairies are excited, except Crystal.
"I'm not so sure," Crystal says quietly.
"But why?" Storm asks. "You love to dance."
"I do like to dance," Crystal agrees. "But
what if I mess up?"

"You'll be fine," Goldie insists. "We'll practise. We're all in this together."
Crystal tries to smile.

Each fairy plans a special dance for her kind of weather.
Then they all work on the grand dance that comes at the end of their ballet.

"We're all in the finale," Hayley says.
"Because it's a gift from all of us."

The fairies start to practise.

They help one another with their dances.
Each one is different, but they all tell a story
about weather.

When it is Crystal's turn, she is nervous.
Before her big leap, she stumbles and falls.

"I'll never get it right," Crystal says with a
sigh. "I can't dance in front of the king and
queen of Fairyland."

Abigail helps the Snow Fairy up.
"Don't worry about them," Evie says.
"When you dance from the heart, you won't
even know the crowd is there."

"I've seen you do that leap hundreds of
times," Hayley says. "You just have to believe
in yourself, like we believe in you."
Crystal nods and starts her dance again.

The Weather Fairies practise and practise.
They also design and sew their costumes.

Then they meet with the fairy orchestra.
A ballet needs music!

The night of the Fairy Godmother's
party arrives.
There is a big outdoor stage.

The guests sit on blankets under the stars.
The Fairy Godmother, King Oberon and
Queen Titania are there.

The Weather Fairies wait backstage for their turn.
Crystal peeks out from behind the curtain and crosses her wings for good luck.

The fairy orchestra starts to play.
Goldie is the first to go on. She does a "Dance
of the Rising Sun." At first, the stage is dark.
Then rays of light burst from Goldie's wand as
she dances.

Pearl bounds in next, flipping from one fluffy cloud to another.

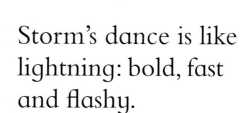

Storm's dance is like lightning: bold, fast and flashy.

Hayley wears rain boots and dances with an umbrella, twirling around and around.

Then Evie dances on to the stage, slow and graceful, like a misty dream.

Abigail wears a crown of acorns, and skips as she throws leaves in the air like the autumn breeze.

The music grows soft.
Giant, glittery snowflakes begin to fall.
Crystal floats on to the stage, whirling around
with the snowflakes.
It's time for her big jump. Crystal leaps into
the air.

When she lands, she's so happy, she glows.

The seven fairies dance on to the stage for the grand finale.
Their wings sparkle under the lights.

The music fills their hearts, and they
pirouette around the stage.
With a swirl of their wands, the sky
lights up with weather magic!

The Weather Fairies bow, and the Fairy
Godmother hurries on to the stage.
"What a beautiful ballet!" she exclaims.
"We did it!" Goldie says to her fairy friends.
Crystal smiles. "Yes, we danced straight from
the heart."